chimpanzee

Printed in the United States of America

First Edition

1 3 5 7 9 10 8 6 4 2

ISBN 978-1-4231-5302-3

For more Disney Press fun, visit www.disneybooks.com

J689-1817-1-12015

Disneynature
chimpanzee

OSCAR AND FREDDY

Adapted by Kristen L. Depken
Photographs by Martyn Colbeck, Mark Linfield, Kristin Mosher, and Bill Wallauer

PRESS
New York

Meet Oscar.

He is a baby chimpanzee.

He lives in a forest in Africa.

Oscar likes to play.
He climbs up tall trees.
He slides down leafy vines.

This is Isha.

She is Oscar's mother.

She takes care of Oscar and teaches
him how to live in the forest.

Oscar stays close to Isha.
He rides on her back
and drinks her milk.
Isha keeps Oscar safe.

Isha teaches Oscar how to eat.
She helps him find nuts.
Then she shows him how
to crack the nuts with a stick.
Oscar tries it himself.

Oscar is too little to crack
nuts on his own.
He needs Isha to help him.
Then he eats one. Yum!

Oscar does not know how to
chew his food.
Isha sticks out her tongue
and shows him the food
in her mouth.

Then Oscar sticks out his tongue!
Oscar learns everything he knows
from his mother.

Oscar and Isha live
with a group of chimpanzees.
They share the fruit, nuts,
and other food they find.

The group is like a big family.
Some chimps are young
like Oscar.
Some are old.

This is Freddy.
He is the leader
of all the chimps in
Oscar and Isha's group.

The other chimpanzees
look up to Freddy.
He is in charge of hunting.
He keeps the group safe.

This is Scar.
He is in charge of another group
of chimpanzees.
They live in the forest near
Freddy, Isha, and Oscar.

Scar's group is big and strong.
They want to steal food from Freddy's
group and take over the forest.
The two groups are rivals.

One night,
Scar's group attacks.
Freddy tries to fight them.
But they are too strong.

In the morning,
Oscar looks for his mother, Isha.
But he cannot find her.
She is gone.
Oscar is all alone.

Oscar stays with his group.
He looks for food to eat.
The group finds honey,
but there is not enough
left for Oscar.

Oscar tries to use a rock
to crack nuts.
But the rock is too heavy for him.
He cannot crack the nuts
by himself.

The other chimpanzee mothers
have babies of their own.
They cannot take care of Oscar, too.
So Oscar turns to Freddy.

Leaders do not usually
take care of baby chimpanzees.
Oscar follows Freddy anyway.
When Freddy eats,
Oscar copies him.

Freddy starts to help Oscar.
He finds honey for Oscar.
He cracks nuts for Oscar.
Now Oscar has food again!

Oscar and Freddy are bonding.
Soon, they spend all their time
together.

Freddy and Oscar eat together.

They play together.

They sleep together.

Freddy takes care of Oscar
just like Isha did.

But then Scar and the
rivals return!
They try to take over one
of Freddy's fruit trees.
Freddy has to stop them.

Freddy takes charge.
He and his group are ready
when Scar and the rivals attack.
Together, they defeat the rivals!
Oscar and Freddy's group is safe.

Now Oscar is bigger.

He finds food for himself.

He uses tools.

He plays with younger chimps.

Thanks to Freddy,
Oscar's group is not
in danger anymore.
Oscar is strong and healthy.

One day,
Oscar may lead a group
of his own—
just like Freddy does.